The Wind in the Willows

By Kenneth Grahame

Retold by Mary Weber
Illustrated by Isidre Mones

Managing Art Editor Tom Gawle
Senior Editor Heather Bazata
Designer Tim Carls

This Book Belongs To:

_____

FREDERIC THOMAS INC.
Produced by: Frederic Thomas Inc., Naples, Florida, Tel: 239-593-8000.

❦ The Riverbank ❦

The Mole had been working very hard all morning, spring-cleaning his little home. First with brooms, then with dusters, last with a brush and a pail of whitewash. His back ached and his arms were weary. Spring was in the air and its delightful call was beckoning the Mole to the meadow. It was small wonder that he suddenly flung down his brush, said "Bother!" and "Hang spring-cleaning!" and bolted up the tunnel and into the bright sunlight.

Jumping off all his four legs at once, in joy of living and the delight of spring, without its cleaning; he ran across the meadow. The sunshine struck hot on his fur, soft breezes caressed his brow. He spent hours rambling along the hedge-rows and running among the fragrant flowers. He thought his happiness was complete when he found himself by the edge of a river. Never in his life had he seen a river.

As he sat on the grass and looked across the water, a dark hole in the bank opposite, just above the water's edge, caught his eye. Dreamily, he considered what a nice snug dwelling-place it would make for an animal with few wants. As he gazed, something bright and small seemed to twinkle, vanish, then twinkle once more like a tiny star. Then it winked at him and showed itself to be an eye; and a small face began to grow up round it, like a frame round a picture.

A brown little face with whiskers.

A grave round face, with the same twinkle in its eye that had first attracted his notice.

Small neat ears and thick silky hair.

It was the Water Rat!

The two animals stood and regarded each other cautiously.

"Hullo, Mole!" said the Water Rat.

"Hello, Rat!" said the Mole.

"Would you like to come over?" inquired the Rat presently.

"Oh, it's all very well to *talk*," said the Mole, rather pettishly, he being new to river and its ways.

The Rat said nothing, but stooped and unfastened a rope; then lightly stepped into a little boat, which the Mole had not seen.

The Rat rowed smartly across the river. "If you've nothing else on hand, let's make a day of it! I have lunch enough for two!" Then he held up his forepaw, helping the Mole step gingerly into the boat. The Mole, to his delight, found himself actually seated in the stern of a real boat.

"How wonderful!" said he, as the Rat shoved off and took to the oars. "Do you know, I've never been in a boat before in all my life." The Mole waggled his fingers and toes from sheer happiness and gave a sigh of full contentment. "*What a day I'm having!*" he said. "So – this – is – a – River!"

"*The* River," corrected the Rat.

"And you really live by the river? What a jolly life!"

"By it and with it and on it and in it," said the Rat. "It's my world, and I don't want any other."

"What lies over *there*?" asked the Mole, waving a paw towards the woodland that darkly framed the water-meadows on one side of the river.

"That? Oh, that's the Wild Wood," said the Rat shortly. "We don't go there very much, we River-Bankers."

"Aren't they – aren't they very *nice* people in there?" said the Mole a trifle nervously.

"W – e – ll," replied the Rat, "let me see. The squirrels are all right. *And* the rabbits. And then there's Badger, of course. He lives right in the heart of it. You must meet him someday. But of course – there – are others," explained the Rat in a hesitating sort of way. "Weasels – and stoats – and ferrets – and so on. They're all right in a way – but they sometimes – well, you can't really trust them."

The Mole knew that it is quite against animal-etiquette to dwell on possible trouble ahead; so he dropped the subject.

"Here's our backwater, where we can lunch," said the Rat.

He brought the boat alongside the bank, secured it, helped the still awkward Mole safely ashore and swung out a luncheon-basket. When all was ready, the Rat said, "Now, pitch in, old fellow!" and the Mole was glad to obey, for he had started his spring-cleaning at a very early hour and had not paused to eat.

"What are you looking at?" said the Rat presently, when the edge of their hunger was somewhat dulled, and the Mole's eyes were able to wander off the food.

"I am looking," said the Mole, "at a streak of bubbles that I see traveling along the surface of the water."

"Bubbles? Oho!" said the Rat, chirruping cheerily in an inviting sort of way.

A broad, glistening muzzle showed itself above the edge of the bank, and the Otter hauled himself out and shook the water from his coat.

"Greedy beggars!" he observed, making for the luncheon-basket. "Why didn't you invite me, Ratty?"

"This was an impromptu affair," explained the Rat. "By the way – my friend, Mr. Mole."

"Proud, I'm sure," said the Otter, and the two animals were friends forthwith.

"Tell us *who's* out on the river, Otter?"

"Toad's out, for one," replied the Otter. "In his brand-new boat; new togs, new everything!"

The Otter and the Rat looked at each other and laughed.

"Once, it was nothing but sailing," said the Rat. "Then he tired of that and took to houseboating. He was going to spend the rest of his life in a houseboat. It's all the same, whatever he takes up; he gets tired of it and starts on something fresh."

An errant Mayfly swerved unsteadily above the water, then there was a swirl of water and a "plop!" The Mayfly was visible no more. Neither was the Otter. But again there was a streak of bubbles on the surface of the river.

The Rat hummed a tune, and the Mole recollected that animal-etiquette forbade any sort of comment on the sudden disappearance of one's friends.

The afternoon sun was getting low as the Rat rowed homewards. "Mole, you and I have had a very nice day. I think it would be good if you could stay with me for a while. My place is plain and rough – not like Toad's house but it's comfortable. And, as a friend, I'll teach you to row and to swim, and you'll soon be as handy on the water as any of us."

The Mole was so touched by this that he could find no voice to answer; and he had to brush away a tear with the back of his paw.

When they got home, the Rat made a bright fire in the parlor and told the Mole river stories till suppertime. Supper was a most cheerful meal; but very shortly afterwards, a terribly sleepy Mole had to be escorted upstairs to the best bedroom, where he soon laid his head on his pillow, knowing that on this day he had made a lifelong friend. ✇

✎ The Open Road ✎

"**R**atty," said the Mole one bright summer morning, "Won't you take me to call on Mr. Toad? I've heard so much about him, and I do so want to meet him."

"Why, certainly," said the good-natured Rat. "We'll get the boat, and paddle there at once."

"Toad is indeed the best of animals," Rat offered, as he rowed the boat. "Perhaps he's not very clever – we can't all be geniuses; and it may be that he is both boastful and conceited. But he has got some great qualities, and he is a friend, nevertheless."

Rounding a bend in the river, they came in sight of a handsome, dignified old house with well-kept lawns reaching down to the water's edge.

"There's Toad Hall," said the Rat. "Toad is rather rich, and this is one of the nicest houses in these parts, though we never admit as much to Toad."

They left the boat and strolled across the lawn in search of Toad, whom they found resting in a garden-chair, with a large map spread out on his knees.

"Hooray!" he cried, jumping up, "This is splendid!" He shook the paws of both of them warmly, never waiting for an introduction to the Mole. "I was just going to send a boat down the river for you, Ratty. You've got to help me!"

"It's about your rowing, I suppose," said the Rat, with an innocent air. "You're getting on fairly well, though you splash a good bit still."

"Oh, pooh! Boating!" interrupted the Toad in great disgust. "Silly boyish amusement. I've given that up *long* ago. No, I've discovered the real thing. Come with me, dear Ratty, and your good friend, also."

He led the way to the stable-yard, the Rat following with a most mistrustful expression; and there they saw a gypsy wagon, shining with newness, painted a canary-yellow with green and red wheels. "There you are!" cried the Toad. "It is fully packed, so we'll harness the horse and start out this very afternoon."

"I beg your pardon," said the Rat slowly, "but did I overhear you say something about '*we*,' and '*start*' and '*this afternoon*'?"

"Now, Ratty," said Toad imploringly, "don't talk in that stiff and sniffy sort of way, because you know you've *got* to come. I can't possibly manage without you."

"I don't care," said the Rat. "I'm not coming and that's flat. And what's more, Mole's going to stick with me and do as I do, aren't you Mole?"

"Of course I am," said the Mole loyally. "I'll always stick to you, Rat. All the same, it sounds as if it might have been, well, rather fun, you know!" he added wistfully.

The Rat saw what was passing in Mole's mind and wavered. He hated to disappoint the Mole. Still unconvinced, he allowed his good nature to override his personal objections.

They had a pleasant ramble that day over grassy downs and along narrow by-lanes. It was late afternoon when they came out on the high road. Mole, walking by the horse's head, and the Toad and the Water Rat, walking next to the

wagon, suddenly heard a faint warning sound behind them. It hummed, like the drone of a distant bee. Watching, they saw a small cloud of dust advancing on them at incredible speed, while from out of the dust a faint "poop-poop!" wailed like an uneasy animal in pain. With a blast of wind and whirl of sound, it passed by them. The "poop-poop" rang with a brazen shout in their ears. They had a moment's glimpse of a magnificent motorcar as it flung up a cloud of dust and then dwindled to a speck in the far distance and changed back into a droning bee once more.

The horse reared and plunged, the straps broke, and the wagon slid backwards towards the deep ditch on the side of the road. It wavered an instant – then there was a heartrending crash – and the canary-colored wagon lay wrecked in the ditch.

The Rat danced up and down in the road. "You villain!" he shouted, shaking both fists. "You scoundrel, you – you – road hog! I'll have the law on you!"

Meanwhile, Toad stared wide-eyed in the direction of the disappearing motorcar. He breathed short, his face wore a satisfied expression, and at intervals, he faintly murmured, "poop-poop."

The Rat grabbed the horse's reins and began to lead the horse down the road. "Come on! The wagon is done," he said grimly to the Mole. "It's five or six miles to the nearest town, and it's best we start out now."

"But what about Toad?" asked the Mole, anxiously. His friend still sat in the road, a happy smile on his face. At intervals he was still heard murmuring, "poop-poop!"

"Oh bother, Toad," said the Rat. "He is now possessed. He'll continue like that for days."

Leading the horse, the Rat and the Mole set off in the direction of town. Soon they heard a pattering of feet behind them. Toad had caught up and thrust a paw inside the elbow of each of them.

"Now, look here, Toad!" said the Rat sharply, "As soon as we get to town, you'll have to go straight to the police station, and see if they know anything about that motorcar, and who it belongs to and lodge a complaint against it."

"Police station! Complaint!" murmured Toad dreamily. "Me *complain* about that beautiful vision!"

The Rat turned from him in despair. "You see?" he said to the Mole. "He's quite hopeless."

On reaching the town, they left the horse at an inn stable and gave directions to find the wagon. A train landed them at a station not far from Toad Hall. They escorted the spellbound Toad home; then got into their boat and rowed home.

The following evening, the Mole was sitting on the bank fishing, when the Rat came strolling along. "Heard the news?" he said. "There's nothing else being talked about, all along the riverbank. Toad went to town by an early train this morning. And he has ordered a large, expensive motorcar." ☛

❧ The Wild Wood ❧

The Mole had long wanted to meet the Badger. When Mole asked if they could visit him, Ratty replied, "He'll be coming along some day, if you'll just wait." The Mole had to be content with this. But the Badger never came.

The days passed, summer left and the cold of winter kept Rat and Mole indoors. In the wintertime, the Rat slept a great deal, retiring early and rising late. Mole had a good deal of spare time on his hands. One afternoon, when the Rat dozed by the fire, the Mole decided to explore the Wild Wood and perhaps visit Mr. Badger.

Slipping out of the warm parlor, the Mole shivered in the cold winter air. The country lay bare and entirely leafless around him. As he entered Wild Wood, twigs crackled under his feet and logs tripped him. Everything was very still. Within the woods, the sun barely shone through the branches, and any light seemed to be draining away like floodwater.

Then the Mole began to see faces, but when he turned, the faces were gone.

Then the whistling began. Very faint and shrill it was and far behind him. It made him hurry forward.

Then the pattering began. He thought it was only falling leaves at first. Then as it grew it took a regular rhythm. In a panic, the Mole began to run. He ran up against things, he fell over things and into things. At last, he took refuge in the dark, deep hollow of an old tree, which offered shelter, concealment and perhaps even safety. As he lay there, panting and trembling, and listened to the whistling and the pattering outside, he knew it at last – the Terror of the Wild Wood!

Meanwhile, the Rat slept. A coal slipped, the fire crackled and sent up a spurt of flame and he woke with a start. He looked round for the Mole, but he was not there. He called, "Moly!" several times, and receiving no answer, got up and went into the hall. There he discovered that the Mole's cap and galoshes were missing.

The Rat left the house and carefully examined the muddy surface of the ground outside. He could see Mole's imprints in the mud, running along straight and purposeful to the Wild Wood. It was getting towards dusk when the Rat reached the first fringe of trees. He plunged into the wood, looking anxiously on either side for any sign of his friend, calling out, "Moly! Moly! Where are you?"

He had patiently hunted through the wood for an hour or more, when at last he heard a little answering cry. He made his way through the gathering darkness to the foot of an old tree with a hole in it, and from out of the hole came a soft voice saying, "Ratty! Is that you?"

The Rat crept into the hollow, and there he found the Mole, exhausted and trembling. "Oh, Rat!" he cried, "I've been so frightened!"

The Rat comforted him (because that's what friends do). "We really must pull ourselves together and make a start for home." By now it was quite dark, and snow was falling. "We must make a start. I don't exactly know where we are, and this snow makes everything look so very different." However, holding on to each other, they set out bravely and took the way that seemed most promising.

But they came to a sudden halt when the Mole tripped and fell. "Oh, my leg!" he cried. "I must have tripped over a stump," said the Mole miserably.

"It's a very clean cut," said the Rat, examining the Mole's wound. "But it wasn't done by a stump. It looks as if it was made by the sharp edge of something. Funny," he pondered, looking at the ground. Seeing something, a metal boot scraper, he scratched furiously at the snow on the hillside. Scrape, scratch, dig! Scrape, scratch, dig! Soon the side of what seemed to be a door appeared. After more digging, an engraved sign was revealed. It read, "MR. BADGER" and to its right hung a bell.

"Ring the bell while I hammer," said the Rat. While he attacked the door with a stick, the Mole sprang up and rang the bell. From quite a long way off they could faintly hear a deep-toned response.

✒ Mr. Badger ✒

Suddenly there was the noise of a bolt shot back, and the door opened a few inches, enough to show a long snout and a pair of sleepy eyes. "Who is disturbing me on such a night? Speak up!"

"Oh, Badger," cried the Rat. "Let us in, please. It's me, Rat, and my friend Mole, and we've lost our way in the snow."

"What, Ratty, my dear little man!" exclaimed the Badger, in quite a different voice. "Come along in, both of you." He opened the door fully and led them to a large fire-lit kitchen.

They removed their wet coats and boots. Then the Badger fetched them dressing gowns and slippers and cleaned the Mole's shin with warm water.

The Badger listened sympathetically as the Mole and Rat told of their terrible visit to the Wild Wood. The Badger nodded and did not interrupt or blame. The Mole began to feel very friendly toward the warm-hearted animal.

Then, as they ate a plentiful meal, talk turned to other matters. "Now then!" said the Badger. "Tell me the news from your part of the world. How's old Toad?"

"Oh, he's from bad to worse," said the Rat gravely. "Another smash-up only last week."

"How many has he had?" asked the Badger gloomily.

"Smashes or machines?" asked the Rat. "Oh well, after all, it's the same thing – with Toad. This is the seventh. He's a hopelessly bad driver." Then more seriously, "Badger, we're his friends – oughtn't we do something?"

"Of course you know I can't do anything *now*," he said rather severely. His two friends nodded, quite understanding his point. No animal, according to the rules of animal-etiquette, is ever expected to do anything strenuous or heroic during the winter.

"You and me and our friend the Mole here," said the Badger, "we'll take Toad seriously in hand once winter has passed. We'll *make* him be a sensible Toad."

The friends went to bed that night thinking about Toad and how they might help him. As they waved their farewell to Badger the next morning, they were happy to finally leave Wild Wood and reach their comfortable home, where they would stay until winter had passed. ✒

Mr. Toad

It was a bright summer morning. The Mole and the Water Rat were finishing breakfast in their little parlor and discussing their plans for the day, when a heavy knock sounded at the door.

"Bother!" said the Rat. "See who it is, Mole."

The Mole went to the door and uttered a cry of surprise. "Mr. Badger!"

The Badger strode heavily into the room. "Toad's hour has come!" he said with great solemnity. "This very morning," continued the Badger, "I learned that another new and exceptionally powerful motorcar would arrive at Toad Hall. You two animals will accompany me to the Toad's home, where we will rescue our friend."

"Right you are!" cried the Rat.

They set off on their mission of mercy, Badger leading the way. They reached the carriage-drive of Toad Hall to find, as the Badger had anticipated, a shiny new motorcar, of great size, painted a bright red (Toad's favorite color). As they neared, the door was flung open, and Mr. Toad, dressed in goggles, cap, gaiters and an enormous overcoat came swaggering toward them, drawing on gloves.

"Hello, fellows!" he cried cheerfully. But his hearty words faltered as he noticed the stern faces of his silent friends.

The Badger strode forward. "Take him inside," he said. Toad was hustled through the front door, struggling and protesting.

"Now, then!" he said to the Toad, when the four of them stood together in the hall. "You knew it must come to this, sooner or later, Toad. You've disregarded all the warnings we've given you. You've given us animals a bad name by your furious driving and your smashes. Independence is all very well, but we animals never allow our friends to make fools of themselves. You will come with me into the den, and there you will hear some facts about yourself; and we'll see whether you come out of that room the same Toad that you went in."

He took Toad firmly by the arm, led him into the den and closed the door behind them.

"*That's* no good!" said the Rat. "*Talking* to Toad'll never cure him. He'll *say* anything."

After some three-quarters of an hour, the door opened, and the Badger reappeared, solemnly leading the dejected Toad. "My friends," said the Badger kindly, "I am pleased to inform you that Toad has seen the error of his ways. He has agreed to give up motorcars forever."

"That is very good news," said the Mole gravely.

"Very good news indeed," observed the Rat uncertainly, "if only – *if* only –" He was looking very hard at Toad as he said this and thought he saw something resembling a twinkle in that animal's sorrowful eye.

"There's only one thing more to be done," continued the Badger. "Say you are sorry for what you've done, and you see the folly of it all."

There was a long pause. Toad looked desperately this way and that, but at last he spoke.

"No!" he said a little sullenly, "I'm *not* sorry. And it wasn't folly at all! It was simply glorious!"

"What?" cried the Badger. "You backsliding animal, didn't you tell me just now, in there –"

"Oh, yes, yes, in *there*," said Toad impatiently. "I'd have said anything in *there*."

"Then you don't promise," said the Badger, "never to touch a motorcar again?"

"Certainly not!" replied Toad emphatically. "On the contrary, I faithfully promise that the very first motorcar I see, 'poop-poop!' off I go in it!"

"Told you so, didn't I?" said the Rat to the Mole.

"Very well, then," said the Badger firmly. "Take him upstairs, you two, and lock him in his bedroom."

"It's for your own good, Toady," said the Rat kindly as he led Toad up the stairs and into his room.

"We'll take care of everything, Toad," said the Mole as he locked the bedroom door.

The three decided that the Toad must be guarded, and they divided watches between them.

One fine morning, the Rat, whose turn it was to go on duty, went upstairs to relieve the Badger and the Mole, who then went out for a walk. Toad was still in bed, but awake, when the Rat entered the bedroom.

"How are you today, old chap?" inquired the Rat cheerfully. "Mole and Badger have gone for a walk. They'll be out till luncheon-time, so you and I will spend a pleasant morning together. So jump up, don't lie there moping."

"Dear, kind Rat," murmured Toad, "how little you realize my condition and how far I am from 'jumping up' now – if ever. If I thought you cared, I'd ask you to fetch the doctor."

"Why, what do you want a doctor for?" asked the Rat, coming closer and examining him.

"Surely you have noticed of late –" murmured Toad. "But no – why should you? Tomorrow, indeed, you may be saying to yourself, 'Oh, if only I had noticed sooner! If only I had done something.'"

"Look here, old man," said the Rat, beginning to get rather alarmed. "Of course I'll fetch the doctor." He hurried from the room, not forgetting, however, to lock the door behind him.

The Toad hopped out of bed as soon as he heard the key turn in the lock. Then he dressed as quickly as possible, all the while laughing. He knotted together the sheets from his bed, and tying one end to the bedpost, dropped the other from the window. He slid lightly to the ground, and, taking the opposite direction from the Rat, marched off whistling a merry tune.

When he reached the Red Lion Inn, he remembered he had not breakfasted. He marched into the inn and ordered his meal.

He was halfway through eating when an only too familiar sound was heard approaching. It made Toad fall, trembling all over. The "poop-poop!" drew nearer and nearer. The car could be heard turning into the inn-yard and then coming to a stop. Presently a party, hungry and talkative, entered the inn. Toad paid his bill and sauntered round quietly to the inn-yard. "There can be no harm in just *looking* at it!" thought Toad.

The car stood in the middle of the yard, quite unattended. "I wonder," he said to himself, "I wonder if this sort of car *starts* easily?" Next moment, hardly knowing how it came about, he found he had hold of the door handle and was turning it. As he started the car, the familiar sound broke forth, and the old passion seized Toad. In the driver's seat, he pulled the lever, swung the car round and tore up the street. ✒

꩜ Toad's Misadventures ꩜

For taking the valuable motorcar and driving too fast, Toad was brought before the judge. "For your misdeeds, I am sending you to Camp Woebegone where you will have time to think about your misadventures and become a good Toad, once again."

So Toad was sent to the camp where he duly pondered his past. He thought of the friends he missed and how his silly actions had taken him away from everything he loved. Toad felt sorry, truly sorry. So when the day of Toad's release dawned, he was certainly a good Toad once again.

Feeling sad, but wiser, Toad nearly skipped through the gates of Camp Woebegone. As his feet moved along the path, it brought him closer and closer to his friends. Now, free at last, he remembered happy times at Toad Hall and his many adventures. "They were not *mis*adventures," he thought. "Indeed!" he snorted aloud. "They were Toad-size adventures!" And despite his sorrow over past "crimes," he still thought himself clever, cunning and smart.

"I am Toad, the handsome, the popular, the successful Toad!" He sang as he walked, getting more and more inflated with every minute.

> The Toad – came – home!
> There was panic in the parlors
> and howling in the halls,
> There was crying in the cow-shed
> and shrieking in the stalls,
> When the Toad – came – home!

"Oh, how clever I am! How clever!" Punching his short arms and kicking up his heels, he danced in circles and hopped and jumped and – PLOP! Before he could say, "Onion Sauce," he found himself head over ears in deep water, rapid water, water that bore him along with a force he could not contend. He rose to the surface and tried to grasp reeds and bushes. But the stream was so strong that it tore them out of his hands. "Oh, my!" gasped poor Toad. "If ever I sing another conceited song" – then down he went, and came up breathless and spluttering. As the swift current carried him, he saw that he was nearing a big dark hole in the bank. As he stared before him into the dark, some bright, small thing shone and twinkled. It moved towards him. As it approached, a face grew up gradually around it. It was a most familiar face! Brown and small, with whiskers. Grave and round, with neat ears and silky hair. It was the Water Rat! ▶

⚶ The Return of Toad ⚶

The Rat put out a neat little brown paw, gripped Toad firmly by the scruff of the neck and gave a pull. Dripping, but happy, Toad found himself with his friend once more.

"Oh, Ratty!" he cried. "I've been through such times since I saw you last. Such trials, such sufferings, and all so nobly borne! Oh, I *am* a smart Toad."

"Toad," said the Water Rat. "Stop swaggering. What an awful fool you've made of yourself. When are you going to be sensible and think of your friends and try and be a credit to them?"

"Quite right, Ratty! How *sound* you always are! I'm going to stroll down to Toad Hall and get into dry clothes of my own. I've had enough adventures. I shall lead a quiet, steady and respectable life."

"Stroll gently down to Toad Hall?" cried the Rat, greatly excited. "What are you talking about? Do you mean to say you *haven't* heard?"

"Heard what?" said Toad, turning rather pale.

"You've heard nothing about the stoats and weasels?"

"The Wild-Wooders?" cried Toad.

" – And how they've taken Toad Hall?" continued the Rat.

Toad leaned his elbows on the table and his chin on his paws, and a large tear welled up in each of his eyes.

"When you – got – into that – that – trouble of yours," said the Rat slowly, "animals took sides. The River-Bankers stuck up for you and said you were badly treated, but the Wild-Wooders said it served you right. And they got very cocky and went about saying you would never come back!"

"But Mole and Badger stood by you through thick and thin. They said you would come back again soon, somehow. So they arranged to move their things into Toad Hall and keep it aired for your return. One dark night a band of weasels, ferrets and stoats broke down the doors and rushed the Mole and the Badger from every side. They threw our two friends out into the cold. And the Wild-Wooders have been living in Toad Hall ever since," continued the Rat.

"Oh, have they!" said the Toad, getting up. "I'll jolly soon see about that!"

"It's no good, Toad!" said the Rat. "Sit back down, you'll only get into trouble. We must do nothing until we hear the latest news from Mole and Badger."

"Oh, yes, of course, Mole and Badger," said Toad lightly. "How have they been, the dear fellows?"

"Well may you ask!" said the Rat. "Those two devoted animals have been watching over your house, keeping a constant eye on the stoats and weasels. You don't deserve to have such true and loyal friends. Some day, when it's too late, you'll be sorry you didn't value them more!"

"I'm an ungrateful beast, I know," sobbed Toad, shedding bitter tears.

A heavy knock on the door startled the penitent Toad. The Rat went straight up to the door, opened it and in walked Mr. Badger and the Mole. Badger came solemnly up to Toad, shook his paw and said, "Welcome home, Toad! Alas! What am I saying? Home, indeed. This is a poor homecoming."

"Fancy having you back again," cried the Mole. "Was your return journey pleasant, Toad?"

The Rat, alarmed, pulled the Mole by the elbow; but it was too late. Toad was puffing and swelling already.

"Pleasant? Oh, no!" he said. "I've courageously traveled alone, day and night and in the worst of conditions only to return to my friends who …"

"Toad, do be quiet, please!" said the Rat. "And don't egg him on, Mole. Tell us what the situation is, and what's best to be done."

"The stoats are on guard outside, and they make the best sentinels in the world," said the Badger.

"Then it's all over," sobbed the Toad, giving up.

"Come, cheer up, Toady!" said the Badger. "There are more ways of getting back a place than taking it by storm. Now, I'm going to tell you a secret. There – is – an – underground – passage," said the Badger impressively, "that leads from the riverbank right up into the middle of Toad Hall."

"Oh, nonsense, Badger!" said Toad. "I know every inch of Toad Hall, inside and out."

"My young friend," said the Badger with great severity. "Your father showed it to me. He told me not to tell you. He said, 'He's a good boy, but he simply cannot hold his tongue. If he's ever in a real fix, you may tell him about the secret passage, but not before.'"

The other animals looked hard at Toad to see how he would take this. Toad was inclined to be sulky at first, but he brightened up immediately as Badger laid out his plan.

"We've discovered that there's going to be a big banquet tonight," Badger continued. "All the weasels and ferrets will be gathered in the dining hall, eating and laughing and carrying on, suspecting nothing. They will trust their excellent sentinels. And that is where the passage comes in. That very useful tunnel leads right up under the butler's pantry, next to the dining room!"

"We shall creep quietly into the butler's pantry – " cried the Mole.

"And rush in upon them," said the Badger. "We've got our work cut out for us, so let us get ready."

When it began to grow dark, the Badger called out, "Follow me!" He led them along the river for a little way and then suddenly swung himself over the edge into a hole in the riverbank, a little above the water. It was cold, dark and damp in the secret passage. They groped and shuffled along, with their ears pricked up till at last the Badger said, "We ought to be pretty nearly under the Hall." They heard over their heads, a confused murmur of sound, as if people were shouting, cheering, stamping on the floor and hammering on tables.

The passage now began to slope upwards; they groped onward a little further, and then the noise broke out again, quite clear this time. They hurried along the passage till it came to a full stop, and they found themselves standing under the trapdoor that led up to the butler's pantry.

The Badger said, "Now, boys, all together!" and they put their shoulders to the trapdoor and heaved it back. Then, hoisting each other up, they found themselves standing in the pantry, with only a door between them and the banquet hall.

"The hour is come! Follow me!" cried Badger. He flung the door wide. The four heroes strode wrathfully into the room. The mighty Badger, his whiskers bristling, Mole, black and grim and shouting an awful war cry and Rat, desperate and determined. Toad, frenzied with excitement and injured pride, swollen to twice his ordinary size, leaping into the air and emitting Toad-whoops that chilled their foes! There were but four friends, but to the panic-stricken weasels, the hall seemed full of monstrous animals, gray, black, brown and yellow. What a squealing and squeaking and a screeching filled the air! Terrified weasels dove under the table and sprang out the windows! Ferrets uttering squeals of terror rushed wildly this way and that, up the chimney, anywhere to get out of reach.

The affair was soon over. Through broken windows, the shrieks of terrified animals escaping across the lawn were borne faintly to their ears. "They've all disappeared by now, one way or another," said the Mole.

After cleaning up the mess and arranging the banquet room, the warriors sat down to a victory meal. They finished the supper in great joy and contentment and retired to rest between clean sheets. ✒

✥ Happily Ever After ✥

After the taking of Toad Hall, the four friends continued to lead their lives, and their friendship remained strong. More heroic feats were likely for the friends. And what of Toad? At times he would continue to be "full of himself," but his friends would keep him in line. And, after all, isn't that what friends are for? To help us be better people and overcome the difficulties we encounter on our way? With the help of his friends, Toad had learned a lot, and he knew in his heart that he was, indeed, an altered Toad. ✑